Will You Fill My Bucket?

Daily Acts of Love Around the World

by Carol McCloud and Karen Wells

Illustrated by Penny Weber

Ferne Press

NORTH
AMERICA

Children around the world ask,

"Will you fill my bucket

and make me happy, too?"

SOUTH
AMERICA

EUROPE

ASIA

AFRICA

"Will you fill my bucket with the love that comes from you?"

AUSTRALIA

"Will you fill my bucket
and kiss me at my nap?"

"Will you fill my bucket
and push me on the swing?"

"Will you fill my bucket
and clap and dance and sing?"

"Will you fill my bucket
and snuggle cheek to cheek?"

"Will you fill my bucket
and take me for a ride?"

"Will you fill my bucket
and hug me in your arms?"

"Will you fill my bucket
and laugh at all my charms?"

"Will you fill my bucket and show me what to do?"

"Yes, I will fill your bucket
and hold you on my lap."

"Yes, I will fill your bucket and kiss you at your nap."

"Yes, I will fill your bucket
and push you on the swing."

"Yes, I will fill your bucket and clap and dance and sing."

"Yes, I will fill your bucket
and snuggle cheek to cheek."

"Yes, I will fill your bucket and play hide-and-go-seek."

"Yes, I will fill your bucket and keep you by my side."

"Yes, I will fill your bucket
and take you for a ride."

"Yes, I will fill your bucket and laugh at all your charms."

"Yes, I will fill your bucket
and show you what to do."

"Yes, I will fill your bucket
and tell you 'I love you.'"

Just listen and you will hear these words...

"I want to fill your bucket
and it fills my bucket, too...

...when I show you that I love you because I truly do."

To those who love children,

Imagine that as a very young child you were never held in someone's arms, never pushed on a swing, never cuddled, never played with or even spoken to. Tragically, the world discovered that this was life for many children in the Socialist Republic of Romania from 1974 to 1989.

Determined to increase his country's population and build its workforce, Romanian president Nicolae Ceausescu's regime forced women to bear children they could not afford to care for, which resulted in an estimated 150,000 babies and children being warehoused in state-run institutions. While basic needs for food and water may have been met, these orphaned children were fundamentally deprived of love, touch, and human affection.

Their buckets were never filled.

We now know that children's buckets, which represent their mental, emotional, and social health, require daily filling with positive affirmation, acknowledgment, and affection. Each invisible bucket is a vitally important part of every human being. The bucket is the very heart and soul of a child, and it is literally created daily through loving interactions with caring people.

Human need for love and affection knows no boundaries; it is the same around the world.

To children, their parents are their first and primary bucket fillers; however, the buckets of the world's little ones can be filled by anyone who makes the choice to take the time to express love, kindness, and interest in a child. In addition to parents, bucket fillers are grandparents, siblings, family members, friends, neighbors, teachers, or anyone who cares for the happiness and well-being of a child. ***Bucket fillers can be found all over the world in clans, tribes, villages, families, schools, places of worship, or wherever loving people come together.***

Every person in the world was born to be loved and to love; therefore, it is our fervent hope that you enjoy the children in your life and fill their buckets with your love. Take every opportunity to play with them and teach them, encourage them and cherish them, and remember to tell them often how much they fill your bucket by being part of your life.

For all the world's children,
Carol McCloud and Karen Wells

In loving memory of Jean Moffett, who lived to hug children

About the Authors

Carol McCloud and Karen Wells have been best friends since the ninth grade when they attended St. Martin School in Detroit, Michigan. Carol is the second oldest of eight children, and Karen is the oldest of eleven. Both have spent many years educating children and adults, teaching life skills and early childhood classes. Their dream is that the importance of Bucket Filling will be understood by parents, caregivers, and teachers around the world. For more information, visit www.bucketfillers101.com.

About the Illustrator

Penny Weber has been illustrating for the children's market since 2007. Her books include *One of Us* from Tilbury House Publishers, *Amazingly Wonderful Things* published by Raven Tree Press, and *Growing Up with a Bucket Full of Happiness: Three Rules for a Happier Life* from Ferne Press. Her work can also be seen among the many titles with such educational publishers as Compass Media and Oxford University Press.

Penny lives in Holbrook, New York, with her husband, Gerard, and their three children, Douglas, Keith, and Erica, who, along with their cat, Tiger, fill her bucket every day. For more information, visit www.pennyweberart.com.

Learn more about bucket filling through our award-winning books that are perfect for home and school, at our website,

www.bucketfillers101.com,

and our free e-newsletter,

BUCKET FILL-OSOPHY 101.

Authors' Acknowledgment:

In the 1960s, Dr. Donald O. Clifton (1924-2003) first created the "Dipper and Bucket" story that has now been passed along for decades. Dr. Clifton later went on to co-author the #1 *New York Times* bestseller *How Full Is Your Bucket?* and was named the Father of Strengths Psychology.

A portion of the proceeds from this book is being donated to help meet the needs of children and families around the world.

Will You Fill My Bucket? Daily Acts of Love Around the World
Copyright © 2012 by Carol McCloud. First Printing, 2012
Illustrations created by Penny Weber with acrylic paint
Book design by Susan Leonard
Printed in Canada on recycled paper

Summary: Children around the world remind us of their need for love and affection by asking us to fill their buckets. Tender responses affirm that bucket filling is the essence of being loved and loving others.

Library of Congress Cataloging-in-Publication Data
McCloud, Carol and Wells, Karen
Will You Fill My Bucket? Daily Acts of Love Around the World/Carol McCloud and Karen Wells–First Edition
ISBN-13: 978-1-933916-98-9 Hardcover
ISBN-13: 978-1-933916-97-2 Softcover
1. Child Development. 2. Parenting. 3. Bucket Filling. 4. Love. 5. Families.
I. McCloud, Carol and Wells, Karen II. Title
Library of Congress Control Number: 2012933926

FERNE PRESS

Ferne Press is an imprint of Nelson Publishing & Marketing
366 Welch Road, Northville, MI 48167
www.nelsonpublishingandmarketing.com